NOODLEHEAD NIGHTMARES

by Tedd Arnold
Martha Hamilton
and Mitch Weiss

illustrated by Tedd Arnold

Holiday House / New York

For Bobbie and Keith—T. A.
In memory of Jeff, whose funny IQ was off the charts—M. H. and M. W.

Authors' Notes—Story Sources for *Noodlehead Nightmares*

The motifs to which we refer in the information that follows are from *The Storyteller's Sourcebook: A Subject, Title, and Motif Index to Folklore Collections for Children* by Margaret Read MacDonald, 1st edition (Detroit: Gale, 1982) and 2nd edition (Detroit: Gale, 2001). Several references are also made to *The Book of Noodles: Stories of Simpletons; or, Fools and Their Follies*, a scholarly work by W. A. Clouston (London: Eliot Stock Publishers, 1888).

What a Nightmare!

The theme of fools not being able to find their own legs is a common one in world folktales. The motif for this story is: *J2021 Numskulls cannot find their own legs*. W. A. Clouston describes Icelandic and Scottish variations on pp. 32–33 of *The Book of Noodles*. Variations of the story written for children can be found in: "The Men with Mixed-Up Feet," in *Noodlehead Stories: World Tales Kids Can Read and Tell* by Martha Hamilton and Mitch Weiss (Atlanta: August House Publishers, 2000); "The Mixed-Up Feet and the Silly Bridegroom," in *Zlateh the Goat and Other Stories* by Isaac Bashevis Singer (New York: Harper & Row, 1966); "How the Twelve Clever Brothers Got Their Feet Mixed Up," in *The Twelve Clever Brothers and Other Fools: Folktales from Russia* by Mirra Ginsburg (NY: J. B. Lippincott, 1979).

The Best Dream

The theme of two characters arguing over food and a trickster settling the fight by dividing it for them, all the while really eating it, is told around the world. We found variations from both Africa and Japan where two cats fight over a piece of cheese and a monkey settles the argument. In a version from Hungary, two bears find a piece of cheese and are tricked by a fox. The motif is: *K452 Unjust umpire misappropriates disputed goods*. Interesting variations include: "Dividing the Cheese," in *Catlore: Tales from Around the World* retold by Marjorie Zaum (NY: Atheneum, 1985); "Dog, Cat, and Monkey," in *The Oxfam Book of Children's Stories: South & North, East & West* edited by Michael Rosen (Cambridge, MA: Candlewick Press, 1992); "The Two Foolish Cats" in *The Sea of Gold: And Other Tales from Japan* adapted by Yoshiko Uchida (NY: Scribner's, 1965); *Two Greedy Bears: Adapted from a Hungarian Folktale* by Mirra Ginsburg (NY: Macmillan, 1976).

Another common theme found in this story is settling an argument over food by agreeing that whoever has the best dream will get to eat the food (motif: *K444 Dream bread: the most wonderful dream*). One character always eats it while everyone else is asleep. In a Navajo story, Coyote, Skunk and Porcupine find a piece of meat and finally agree that whoever has the most beautiful dream will get to eat it all by himself. That is exactly what Porcupine does while the others are napping. Variations can be found in: "The Beautiful Dream," in *Stories in My Pocket: Tales Kids Can Tell* by Martha Hamilton and Mitch Weiss (Golden, CO: Fulcrum Publishing, 1996); "Three Dreams," in *Noodles, Nitwits, and Numskulls* by Maria Leach (New York: Scholastic, 1961).

Bedtime for Noodleheads

The inspiration for this story came from two tiny noodle tales from ancient Greece described by W. A. Clouston in *The Book of Noodles*. In one story, a man dreams that he got a nail in his foot and decides that he should never sleep barefoot again (p. 6) (motif: *F1068.5 Fool dreams he hurt foot*). In the other, a fool uses a jar as a pillow after putting feathers inside because he thinks the feathers would make the jar soft (pp. 5–6). A similar story from Ireland, "The Fool's Feather Pillow," can be found in *Noodlehead Stories: World Tales Kids Can Read and Tell* by Martha Hamilton and Mitch Weiss (Atlanta: August House Publishers, 2000).

Text copyright © 2016 by Tedd Arnold, Martha Hamilton and Mitch Weiss
Illustrations copyright © 2016 by Tedd Arnold
All Rights Reserved
HOLIDAY HOUSE is registered in the U.S. Patent and Trademark Office.
Printed and Bound in October 2016 at Toppan Leefung Printing Co., Ltd., DongGuan City, China.
The artwork was rendered digitally using Photoshop software.
www.holidayhouse.com
3 5 7 9 10 8 6 4 2
Library of Congress Cataloging-in-Publication Data
Arnold, Tedd, author, illustrator.
[Short stories. Selections]
Noodlehead nightmares / by Tedd Arnold, Martha Hamilton and Mitch Weiss ; illustrated by Tedd Arnold.
— First edition.
pages cm
Summary: Brothers Mac and Mac star in this collection of bedtime tales inspired by folktales about fools from around the world.
ISBN 978-0-8234-3566-1 (hardcover)
[1. Fools and jesters—Fiction. 2. Bedtime—Fiction. 3. Brothers—Fiction. 4. Humorous stories.]
I. Hamilton, Martha, author. II. Weiss, Mitch, 1951- author. III. Title.
PZ7.A7379Ns 2016
[E]—dc23
2015022726
ISBN 978-0-8234-3768-9 (paperback)

You can tell we're Noodleheads by looking at us—because, well, we **are** noodles. But we're harder to spot if we wear hats.

Now we are totally disguised.

Hey, look! It's Farmer Spud.

NOODLEHEAD NIGHTMARES

CHAPTER 1
WHAT A NIGHTMARE!

One night, Mac and Mac made an announcement to their mother.

NOODLEHEAD NIGHTMARES

CHAPTER 2
THE BEST DREAM

My dream was good. I dreamed I ate a thousand pies.

My dream was better. I dreamed I ate a million pies.

My dream was best. I dreamed I ate one pie.

How can your dream be best if you only ate one pie?

NOODLEHEAD NIGHTMARES

CHAPTER 3

BEDTIME FOR NOODLEHEADS

Mac was not comfortable, but he was tired.

He tossed and he turned, and finally he slept.

Mac and Mac slept until morning.

Time to make our beds.

Yes, and I have an idea.

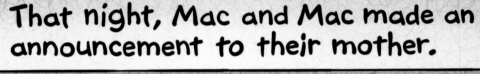

That night, Mac and Mac made an announcement to their mother.

We aren't making our beds anymore.

And how is that?